To our new crew: Ann, Obie and Nate ~ P. T.

For Jenna ~ J.

First published 2019 by Walker Books Ltd, 87 Vauxhall Walk, London SE11 5HJ · This edition published 2020 · Text © 2019 Patricia Toht
Illustrations © 2019 Jarvis · The right of Patricia Toht and Jarvis to be identified as author and illustrator respectively of this work has been asserted
by them in accordance with the Copyright, Designs and Patents Act 1988 · This book has been typeset in OPTIMemphis · Printed in China
British Library Cataloguing in Publication Data: a catalogue record for this book is available from the British Library
ISBN 978-1-4063-9297-5 · www.walker.co.uk · 10 9 8 7 6 5 4 3 2 1

This Walker book belongs to:

....

....

....

PICK A PUMPKIN

Patricia Toht   illustrated by Jarvis

WALKER BOOKS
AND SUBSIDIARIES
LONDON · BOSTON · SYDNEY · AUCKLAND

Pick a pumpkin
from the patch —

tall and lean,
or short and fat.

Vivid orange,
ghostly white,
or speckled green
might be just right.

Pumpkin snugly
in your arms,
wheel a wagon
through the farm.

Stop for mugs
of spicy punch,
toffee apples,
sweet to crunch.

Homeward from
the pumpkin patch,
all your goodies
stacked in back.

Now...

Brush or wipe your pumpkin clean.
Rub it smooth and make it gleam.

Find the perfect carving space,
lined with papers just in case
you make a mess.

Next...

Gather other
things you need:
a bowl, a spoon
for scooping seeds,

a tool to trace
a spooky face,
and plastic saws
for cutting shapes.

Then...

Invite around
a friend or two —

form a
PUMPKIN
CARVING
CREW!

Let grown-ups cut the top a bit,
big enough for hands to fit.
Reach down deep into the hole,
grab the seeds and give a pull.

Lumpy chunks. Sticky strings.
Clumpy seeds. Guts and things.
With a spoon, scrape sides neatly.
Clean the inside out completely.

Now all together...

Carve the eyes.
Giant circles of surprise.
Small slits sleeping
or one eye peeping.
Cross-eyed crazy.
Angry. Lazy.

And below those ...

make a nose.
A triangle. A pinprick.
A nose that grows
from thin to thick.

Under the nose...

Is where the mouth goes.
A kiss. A frown.
A toothy grin.
A zigzag gap
cut long and thin.

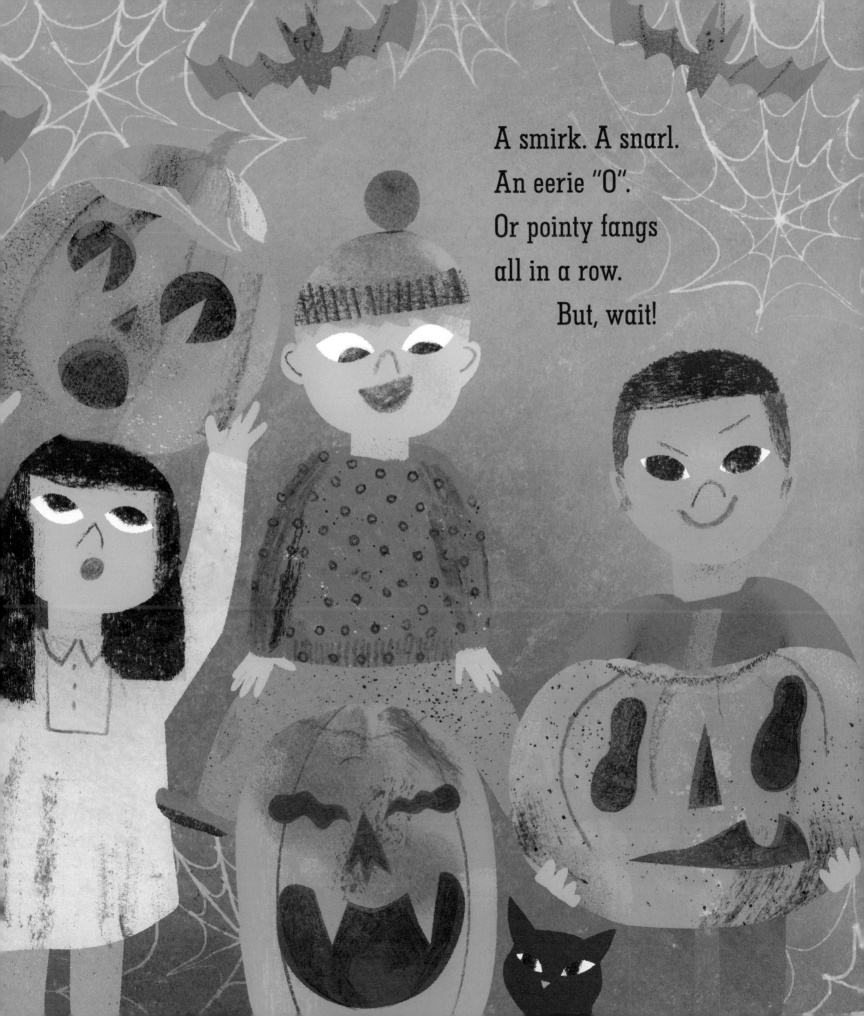

A smirk. A snarl.
An eerie "O".
Or pointy fangs
all in a row.
But, wait!

Before you light your new creation,
first it's time for decorations!

Cobwebs strung from post to post.
Rings of gauzy dancing ghosts.
Spiders. Tombstones.
Dangling bats.
Skeletons and witches' hats.

Now quick!
Slip on gear
to trick or treat,
and grab a sack
to hold your sweets.

Lift your pumpkin up with pride.
March it to a place outside.
Set it safely on the ground,
and call the crew
to gather round.

Ask someone to strike a match.
Watch! The candle's wick
will catch.

See it glow outside your door.

LOOK!
It's not a pumpkin
any more.

It's a...

JACK-O'-LANTERN!

Its red-hot eyes
will gaze
and flicker.

Its fiery grin
will blaze and snicker,
to guard your house
while you have fun...

Happy Halloween,

everyone!

Look out for:

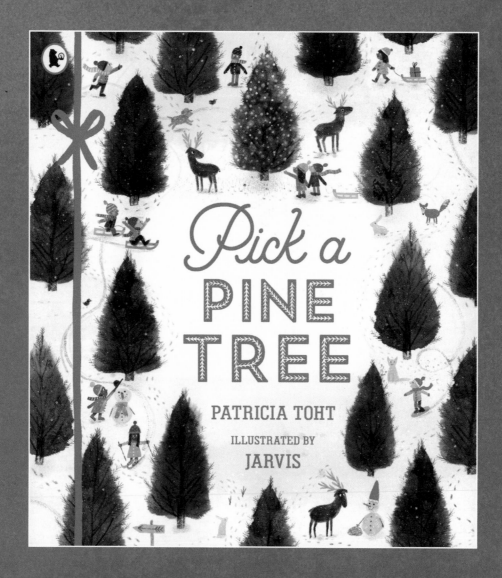

"Everyone in the soft-glowing images is beaming ... by the end of the book, readers will be, too" *Guardian, The Best Children's Books of 2017*

"A sprightly, unashamedly Christmassy book" *Observer*

"If you're going to pick a Christmas book, you'll struggle to find one more festively atmospheric" *The Herald*

Available from all good booksellers

www.walker.co.uk